Every day for a week, Neville had brought the crab man six hermit crabs. And every day Neville had taken home a U.S. dollar. Even though Neville's father worked in the sugar cane fields, there was little money for extras.

Neville was saving his crab money to buy a new dress for his mother. But when he learns that the crab man is mistreating the crabs, he must choose between helping his family to make ends meet and protecting the environment.

The story, "The Crab Man," was awarded 'First Place for Children's Fiction' by the Oklahoma National League of American Pen Women.

PRINTED AND BOUND
IN THE UNITED STATES OF AMERICA

Ages 4 and up

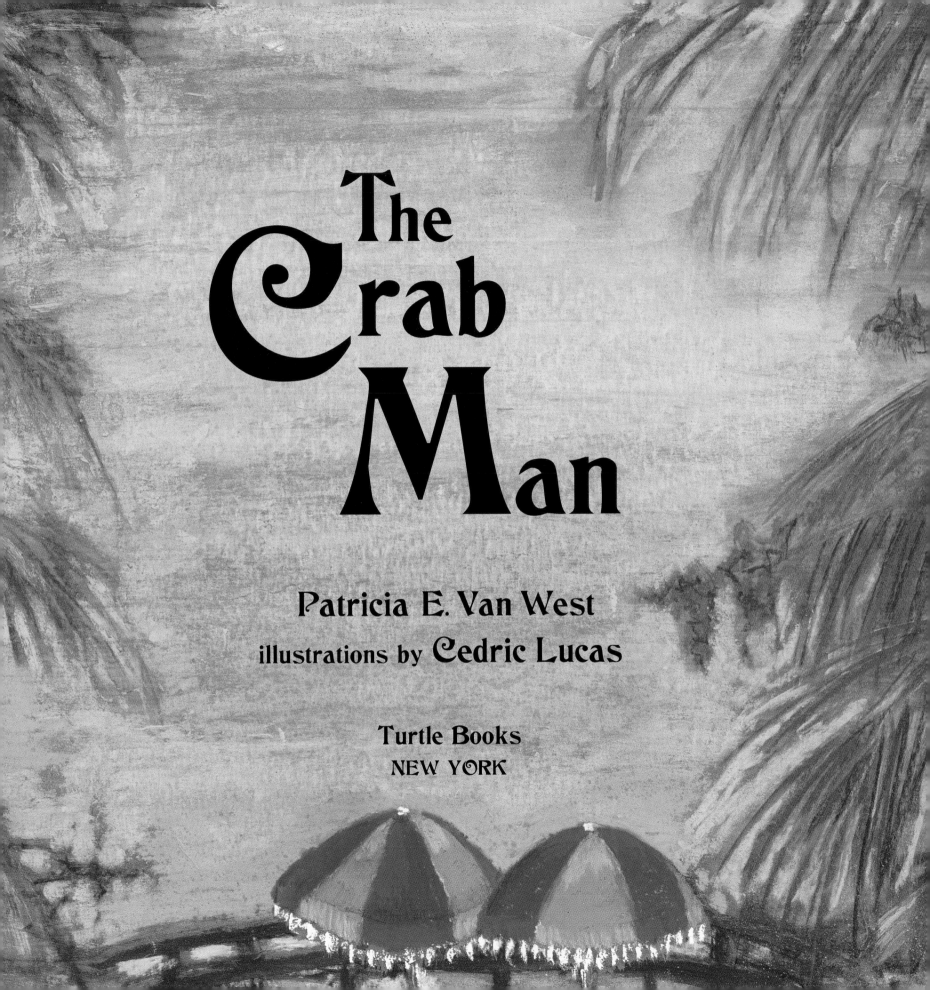

The Crab Man

Patricia E. Van West

illustrations by Cedric Lucas

Turtle Books
NEW YORK

"Gotcha,"
Neville said as he reached
into the bush and snatched
up a small brown object. It
tickled his hand as it tried to
escape, but Neville held on.
Gently, he lowered it into the shoe
box with the other three hermit crabs.
Two more to go.

The boy spent the next half hour
searching the bushes until the last two crabs
were captured. Then using an old piece of
screen as a lid, he headed off to meet the
crab man.

From a distance Neville could see the crab man standing in front of the hotel gate talking to the guard. Inside the gates, a group of tourists was boarding a bus.

Perhaps these tourists would climb Dunn's River Falls or go rafting down the Martha Brae River. They might even tour the sugar cane plantation where Neville's father worked. The island of Jamaica depended on tourists. And now Neville depended on them, too.

"Six?" the crab man asked as Neville approached.

Neville nodded as he handed over the box.

The crab man lifted the screen and started poking and jabbing each crab. When he was satisfied, he picked up an old black gym bag and dumped the crabs inside. Then he reached into his pocket and handed a crumpled U.S. dollar to Neville.

Every day for a week, Neville had brought the crab man six crabs. And every day, Neville had taken home a U.S. dollar. Even though Neville's father worked in the sugar cane fields, there was little money for extras. Neville was saving his crab money to buy a new dress for his mother—a fancy one the color of the sea.

Still, Neville worried about his crabs. They were his friends. He loved to sit as still as a rock and watch them scamper in the dirt. Sometimes they would crawl over his bare feet and tickle so much that his loud laughter sent them darting into their shells.

The following day, after Neville handed over six more crabs, the crab man said, "My helper's sick. Do his work and I'll pay you an extra dollar." Then the crab man hurried toward the gates of the hotel.

Not only did Neville want the dollar, but he
was curious to go through the hotel gates. As he
hurried after the crab man, the guard reached out
to stop Neville. But one nod from the crab man and
suddenly Neville had entered the hotel grounds.

Crossing a grove of coconut trees, Neville
saw a gigantic swimming pool surrounded by
lounge chairs and tourists. It was there the crab
man stopped, lowering his gym bag beside a
large, white circle painted on the concrete deck.

"Place your bets, place your bets. It's time
for c-r-r-r-ab r-r-r-r-acing," announced the crab
man in a loud voice.

Tourists wandered toward the circle.

"Here," said the crab man thrusting a small dirty box into Neville's hands. "Dump these crabs in the center of the circle when I say 'go.'"

Reaching the middle of the circle, Neville lifted the lid of the airless box and peered inside. There were six crabs, tucked tightly in their shells. Not dull, brown shells, but brightly painted shells: blue, red, yellow, green, silver, and orange.

"Pick your color! Pick your color!" shouted the crab man. Tourists lined up to place their bets. Then they gathered around the circle, waiting for the race to begin.

The crab man gave Neville the signal.
Neville shook the crabs onto the hot concrete as
gently as he could and backed away. People
cheered as the red crab began to crawl toward
the circle's edge. Soon the other crabs began to
move and more cheers were heard.

"Go blue!" shouted one woman.
"Come on, red!" yelled two young boys.
"Hi ho, silver," said a man as the silver crab neared the finish line.

"**S-i-l-l-l-ver** wins," announced the crab
man. The winners collected their money as
Neville gathered the hot, tired crabs into his
own box with its airier, wire-mesh lid. He knew
they needed water and shade and was looking
for a cool spot to put them when he heard,
"Place your bets. Place your bets. There's more
c-r-r-r-r-ab r-r-r-r-acing."

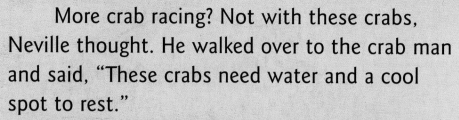

More crab racing? Not with these crabs,
Neville thought. He walked over to the crab man
and said, "These crabs need water and a cool
spot to rest."

"Chuh mon," said the crab man with a
wave of his hand. "They're good for at least four
more races."

Four more races! Neville's hands turned icy
cold under the June sun.

Clutching the box of crabs to his chest, Neville started to run.

"Stop, mon!"

But it was too late. Neville dashed around the pool, past the staring tourists, through the grove of coconut trees, and out the gates of the hotel before the guard could stop him. On and on he ran, until he was safely home.

Neville rushed into the house. Throwing his
arms around his mother, he told her the story.
Wiping his tears, she asked, "What will you do?"

"If I stop selling crabs, I won't be able to
buy you a new dress," said Neville.

"I like crabs more than new dresses," his
mother said with a gentle smile.

Neville thought a moment. Then he hugged his mother before heading outside with the box of crabs. In the cool shade of the bushes, he opened the lid. One at a time, out they came, slowly but surely.

"Its time for c-r-r-r-r-ab r-r-r-r-acing," he whispered as the brightly painted crabs crawled across the dirt and into the bushes.

Author's Notes

Jamaica

The setting of *The Crab Man* is Jamaica. Jamaica, the third largest island in the Caribbean Sea, is slightly smaller than the state of Connecticut. Its climate is hot and tropical. This island is a popular tourist spot because of its rugged mountains, tropical forests, magnificent waterfalls, and miles of white sand beaches. In addition to tourism, many Jamaicans are employed in agriculture (sugar, spices, and fruit) and mining (bauxite and alumina). Although the Jamaican people come from a variety of cultures, they all share the Jamaican motto: "Out of Many, One People."

Hermit Crabs

Hermit crabs begin their lives as larva, swimming in the ocean. After they grow legs, eyes, and body parts, they walk around the ocean floor looking for empty shells to use as houses. After finding the perfect home, they journey to shore. It only takes a few weeks on dry land for hermit crabs to forget how to swim and metamorphose (change) into air-breathing animals.

While they may be small, hermit crabs benefit the environment in a big way. Using other creatures' empty shells makes them the perfect recyclers. In addition, hermit crabs clean up the shoreline by eating creatures that have died. Humans are the crabs' most dangerous enemy because they can pollute the crabs' environment, destroy their habitat, and collect them to sell in pet stores.

For my daughter, Kate— PV

To Diane, Jorrell, Jaleesa; to all who inspire— CL

Turtle
B O O K S

The Crab Man

Text copyright © 1998 by Patricia E. Van West
Illustrations copyright © 1998 by Cedric Lucas

First Hardcover Edition Published in 1998 by Turtle Books
First Softcover Edition Published in 2001 by Turtle Books

Turtle Books, 866 United Nations Plaza, Suite 525
New York, New York 10017

Cover and book design by Jessica Kirchoff
Text of this book is set in Goudy Sans Medium
Illustrations are composed of pastel and casein on marble dust paper

First Softcover Edition
Printed on 80# White Mountie matte, acid-free paper
Printed and bound at Worzalla in Stevens Point, Wisconsin/U.S.A.

10 9 8 7 6 5 4 3 2 1

Library of Congress Cataloging-in-Publication Data
Van West, Patricia E., 1952-
The Crab Man / Patricia E. Van West ; illustrated by Cedric Lucas.   p. cm.
Summary: When Neville sees the hermit crabs which he so gently collected
being mistreated by the crab man at a Jamaican hotel, he no longer
wants to supply them but would thereby forfeit his income.
ISBN 1-890515-25-6 (softcover : alk. paper)
[1. Hermit crabs—Fiction. 2. Crabs—Fiction. 3. Animals—Treatment—Fiction. 4. Jamaica—Fiction.]
I. Lucas, Cedric, ill. II. Title. PZ7.V383Cr 1998 [E]—dc21 98-9679 CIP AC

Distributed by Publishers Group West

ISBN 1-890515-25-6

PATRICIA E. VAN WEST

was born in Amsterdam, the Netherlands and immigrated to the United States with her parents and grandparents when she was two years old. She earned B.S., M.S., and Ed.D. degrees from Illinois State University. Over the past decade, Patricia has taught creative writing courses and workshops to children and adults. She has over 100 publications in magazines, newspapers, and journals. *The Crab Man* is her first children's picture book. Patricia lives in central Illinois with her husband and daughter.

CEDRIC LUCAS was born

in New York City in 1962. He holds a Bachelor of Fine Arts degree from the School of Visual Arts and a Master of Fine Arts degree from Lehman College. Cedric currently teaches art at a New York City middle school. The children's books Cedric has illustrated include: *Frederick Douglass: The Last Day of Slavery; Big Wind Coming; Sugar Cakes Cyril;* and *What's in Aunt Mary's Room.* Cedric has received the New Talent Award from the Art Directors Club and the Gyo Fujikawa Award from the Society of Illustrators. Cedric lives with his wife and two children in Yonkers, New York.

Distributed by
Publishers Group West

The Crab Man is also available in—
a hardcover English edition:
The Crab Man (ISBN: 1-890515-08-6),
a hardcover Spanish edition:
El hombre de los cangrejos (ISBN: 1-890515-09-4),
and a softcover Spanish edition:
El hombre de los cangrejos (ISBN: 1-890515-26-4).

Visit our home page on the World Wide Web:
www.turtlebooks.com

Turtle
BOOKS

866 United Nations Plaza, Suite 525
New York, New York 10017